FOLK HEROES

Betsy Ross

JACQUELINE S. COTTON

MEDIA ENHANCED BOOKS
AV2 BY WEIGL
ADDED VALUE • AUDIO VISUAL
www.av2books.com

Published by AV^2 by Weigl
350 5th Avenue, 59th Floor
New York, NY 10118
Website: www.av2books.com

Library of Congress Cataloging-in-Publication Data
Names: Cotton, Jacqueline S., author.
Title: Betsy Ross / Jacqueline S. Cotton.
Description: New York, NY : AV2 by Weigl, [2020] | Series: Folk heroes | Includes index. | Audience: Grades 4-6. | Audience: Age 9.
Identifiers: LCCN 2019006891| ISBN 9781489695543 (hbk. : alk. paper) | ISBN 9781489695550 (pbk. : alk. paper) | ISBN 9781489695567 (multi-user ebook) | ISBN 9781489695574 (single user ebook)
Subjects: LCSH: Ross, Betsy, 1752-1836--Juvenile literature. | Revolutionaries--United States--Biography--Juvenile literature. | United States--History--Revolution, 1775-1783--Flags--Juvenile literature. | Flags--United States--History--18th century--Juvenile literature.
Classification: LCC E302.6.R77 C68 2020 | DDC 973.3092 [B] --dc23
LC record available at https://lccn.loc.gov/2019006891

Printed in Guangzhou, China
1 2 3 4 5 6 7 8 9 0 23 22 21 20 19

042019
103118

Project Coordinator: Heather Kissock
Art Director: Terry Paulhus

Photo Credits
Weigl acknowledges Getty Images, Alamy, and iStock as its primary image suppliers for this title.

Betsy Ross

CONTENTS

A Legendary Flag Maker

Legend has long said that Betsy Ross made the first American flag. People often tell a story about General George Washington visiting Betsy at her **upholstery** shop. There, he asked her to make a flag that would represent the 13 **colonies** that fought for independence from Great Britain.

As a **Patriot**, Betsy supported the colonies. For this reason, she agreed to make the flag for General Washington. This flag is said to have been the country's first official flag.

The first official American flag was called the "Stars and Stripes."

Betsy Ross is sometimes called the "Mother of America's Flag."

When Betsy was born, Philadelphia was one of the largest cities in colonial America. Approximately 15,000 people lived there.

Growing Up

Betsy Ross was born Elizabeth Griscom on January 1, 1752. She grew up in Philadelphia, Pennsylvania. Betsy's parents, Samuel and Rebecca Griscom, were members of the **Quaker** religion. Like many Quakers, the Griscoms had a large family. Betsy was the eighth of seventeen children.

Growing up in the Quaker faith, Betsy was not allowed to do some of the things that other colonial children could do. She could not read storybooks, dance, or play music. However, as a Quaker, Betsy could attend a formal school. This is something many colonial girls were not allowed to do.

Betsy attended the Friends Public School. She learned how to read, write, and sew. Betsy completed her schooling when she was 12 years old.

Needles and Threads

After Betsy completed school, she worked as an **apprentice** at an upholstery shop. Betsy spent several years at the shop. There, she learned how to make and repair tablecloths, curtains, umbrellas, bedspreads, and chair covers.

In 1773, Betsy married John Ross, another apprentice who worked at the same shop. The couple opened their own upholstery shop soon after. They worked long hours to make their business succeed. When John died in 1776, Betsy ran the upholstery business alone.

Betsy and John had to **elope** to get married. This is because they were not of the same faith.

Today, the house where Betsy and John lived is a museum. People can visit it to learn more about Betsy and life in the colonies.

General Washington is believed to have come to Betsy's house in the summer of 1776.

A Historical Task

General George Washington is said to have visited Betsy at her upholstery shop. He showed her a sketch of a flag made up of six-pointed stars and red and white stripes. He asked her to make a flag based on the sketch.

Although Betsy agreed to make the flag, she suggested that the stars have five points. She explained that five-pointed stars were quicker to cut. After Betsy cut out a five-pointed star for General Washington, he agreed to the change.

Betsy is said to have cut out a five-pointed star with a single snip of her scissors.

Stars and Stripes

The U.S. **Congress** adopted the Stars and Stripes as the country's official flag in 1777. The flag became a symbol of the country's independence. The flag has changed over the years. Today, it has 50 stars on it. A new star has been added every time a state joined the country.

Think About It

The American flag is one of the country's most important symbols. Why does the United States need to have a national flag? What does the flag represent to Americans? What does it tell people from other countries about the United States?

The circle of stars in the blue field represented a new **constellation**. The number of stars represented the union of the colonies.

The alternating red and white stripes on the flag represented the original 13 colonies. These were Delaware, Pennsylvania, New Jersey, Georgia, Connecticut, Massachusetts, Maryland, South Carolina, New Hampshire, Virginia, New York, North Carolina, and Rhode Island.

The rectangular shape of the flag allowed it to wave in the wind. The shape also allowed people to better see the flag from a distance.

The colors of the flag are symbolic. White stands for purity. Red represents strength. Blue stands for justice.

The Ross family told the Historical Society that General Washington chose Betsy to make the flag because they already knew each other and were friends.

The Story Unfolds

Betsy died in 1836. In 1870, Betsy's grandson William Canby told her story to the Historical Society of Pennsylvania. He claimed that his grandmother made the first American flag. Canby presented statements from Betsy's family as **proof**. The family all agreed that Betsy told them stories about making the flag for General Washington.

After Canby's meeting with the society, the story of Betsy Ross quickly spread. People accepted that it was true. Many schools began to include Betsy Ross in their history textbooks.

Today, many **historians** dispute Canby's story about his grandmother. According to them, no **credible** proof exists to confirm that Betsy Ross made the first American flag.

Honoring Betsy

Every year, thousands of people flock to the Betsy Ross House in Philadelphia. This house is said to be the place where Betsy lived when she made the first American flag. People who tour the house can learn more about the life and times of Betsy Ross.

In 1976, the Betsy Ross Bridge opened in Philadelphia. The bridge connects the city to Pennsauken, New Jersey. The Betsy Ross Bridge is one of only a few bridges named after a woman.

Betsy never owned the Betsy Ross House. She lived there as a renter from 1776 to 1779.

Visitors to the Betsy Ross House can ask questions about the flag she made.

Timeline of Betsy Ross

1752
Betsy Ross is born. She grows up in Philadelphia, Pennsylvania.

1764
Betsy finishes school at age 12.

1773
Betsy marries John Ross. They open an upholstery shop.

1782
John Ashburn dies. Betsy marries John Claypoole the following year.

1776
George Washington asks Betsy to make a flag that represents the new nation. Betsy's husband dies.

1777
Betsy's flag becomes the official flag of the United States of America. Betsy marries Joseph Ashburn.

Betsy Ross was a simple tradesperson who was asked to help create a flag for a new nation. Her sewing skills are said to have led to the country's first flag. Betsy has become an American folk hero because of her role in this historic moment.

1827
Betsy retires from the flag-making business. She is 76 years old.

1836
Betsy dies at the age of 84.

1870
Betsy's grandson William Canby tells the Historical Society of Pennsylvania that his grandmother made the first American flag.

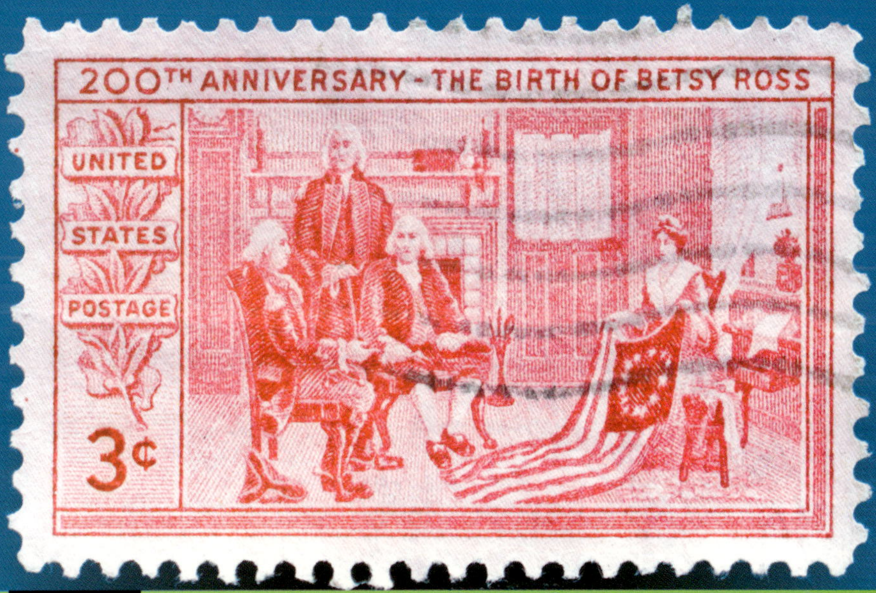

1952
Betsy is featured on a postage stamp. The stamp honors her 200th birthday.

What Have You Learned?

Test your knowledge of Betsy Ross by answering the following questions.

1

What type of business did Betsy and John Ross have?

a) a bakery
b) an upholstery shop
c) a general store
d) a print shop

2

True or False?
Abraham Lincoln asked Betsy to make the American flag.

3

What do the 13 red and white stripes on the flag represent?

a) colonies
b) planets
c) generals
d) cities

4

True or False?
Betsy was married three times.

5

How many brothers and sisters did Betsy have?

a) 15
b) 7
c) 16
d) 11

6

True or False?
There is a bridge in Philadelphia named after Betsy.

7

What age was Betsy when she retired from making flags?

a) 72
b) 65
c) 84
d) 76

8

True or False?
The Stars and Stripes became the official flag of the United States in 1788.

9

What name was Betsy given at birth?

a) Elizabeth Griscom
b) Betsy Ross
c) Elizabeth Grisby
d) Betsy Griscom

10

True or False?
The American flag has six-pointed stars.

ANSWERS

1 b) 2 False. According to legend, George Washington asked her to make the flag. 3 a) 4 True 5 c) 6 True 7 d) 8 False. The Stars and Stripes became the official flag in 1777. 9 a) 10 False. It has five-pointed stars.

Make a Betsy Ross Star

Betsy Ross's five-pointed star has become a key symbol for the United States of America. You can create your own Betsy Ross stars by following the instructions below.

Items Needed:

- a square piece of paper
- scissors

Instructions:

1. Fold the piece of paper in half from left to right.
2. Fold the top left corner down to the center of the bottom edge. You should see a triangle on the left.
3. Fold the triangle up.
4. Fold the triangle up again until it meets the edge of the paper. The paper should be shaped like a waffle cone.
5. With the pointed end of the paper up, cut diagonally from one edge to the next. You may have to experiment with different angles to get a more pointed star.
6. Unfold. Now, you have made a Betsy Ross star.

Key Words

apprentice: a person who learns a trade by working for someone with experience in the trade

colonies: lands ruled by another nation

Congress: the branch of the U.S. government that makes laws

constellation: a group of stars that form a pattern in the sky

credible: able to be believed

elope: to run away secretly to get married

historians: people who study or write about history

legend: a story from the past that cannot be proven true

Patriot: a person who sided with the colonies during the U.S. War of Independence

proof: information that shows something to be true

Quaker: a person who belongs to a religious group that believes in a simple, peaceful life

upholstery: the work of providing furniture, especially seats, with padding and covers

Index

Log on to www.av2books.com

AV² by Weigl brings you media enhanced books that support active learning. Go to www.av2books.com, and enter the special code found on page 2 of this book. You will gain access to enriched and enhanced content that supplements and complements this book. Content includes video, audio, weblinks, quizzes, a slideshow, and activities.

AV² Online Navigation

Book Pages
AV² pages directly correspond to pages in the book.

Audio
Listen to sections of the book read aloud.

Video
Watch informative video clips.

Embedded Weblinks
Gain additional information for research.

Key Words
Study vocabulary, and complete a matching word activity.

Try This!
Complete activities and hands-on experiments.

Quizzes
Test your knowledge.

Slideshow
View images and captions, and prepare a presentation.

AV² was built to bridge the gap between print and digital. We encourage you to tell us what you like and what you want to see in the future.

Sign up to be an AV² Ambassador at www.av2books.com/ambassador.

Due to the dynamic nature of the internet, some of the URLs and activities provided as part of AV² by Weigl may have changed or ceased to exist. AV² by Weigl accepts no responsibility for any such changes. All media enhanced books are regularly monitored to update addresses and sites in a timely manner. Contact AV² by Weigl at 1-866-649-3445 or av2books@weigl.com with any questions, comments, or feedback.